Remembering Barkley

Erin Frankel
illustrated by Aboo Yang

Albert Whitman & Company
Chicago, Illinois

For Bear and Pumpkin. And those who sing in our hearts, forever—EF

To my cat, Hana. I hope you can stay with me for another 10 years.—AY

Library of Congress Cataloging-in-Publication data is on file
with the publisher.
Text copyright © 2020 by Erin Frankel
Illustrations copyright © 2020 by Albert Whitman & Company
Illustrations by Aboo Yang
First published in the United States of America
in 2020 by Albert Whitman & Company
ISBN 978-0-8075-9448-3 (hardcover)
ISBN 978-0-8075-9449-0 (ebook)

Printed in China

10 9 8 7 6 5 4 3 2 1 WKT 24 23 22 21 20

Design by Valerie Hernández

For more information about Albert Whitman & Company,
visit our website at www.albertwhitman.com.

You didn't come back today.
I waited.

But you weren't here the next day either.

Our walk wasn't the same without you.
I didn't feel like running anywhere.

And Jacob wasn't in a hurry.

Jacob threw the ball out into the lake.
Our ball.

I watched it float away.

"Barkley isn't coming back, Bear."

I stopped at your favorite tree. The one you would lie
under to watch the birds when you were too tired to play.
I tried to find you.

I hadn't thought to look for you up there.

For a while, Jacob pulled me quickly
whenever we passed the tree. *Your* tree.

"C'mon, Bear. Let's keep going."
And that is what we did. We kept going.

We tried other paths.
But we missed the old places.

Our places. And my tail didn't move in circles anymore.

One day, when Jacob threw the ball,
I fetched it and ran to the tree. *Your* tree.

"Bring the ball back, Bear.
Bring it back!"

Jacob's face was the color of my leash.

"Bring HIM back!" he hollered as he came toward me.

Then Jacob sat down next to me.
I felt a gentle raindrop on my head.
Jacob was raining!

I let the ball go.
"I miss him too, Bear."

The wind swept the ball away. But we didn't leave. We sat. And listened.
A bird in the tree sang louder than the whistle of the breeze.

We stayed until the bird flew away and took the wind with him.

We came back to your tree. We watched your birds. And kept your spot warm.

And some days Jacob rained.
But *one* day...

"Go fetch, Bear!"

The water felt cool. I felt good.
And Jacob laughed.
Jacob laughed!

I could see the tree. *Your* tree. *Our* tree.

I pictured you there.
Smiling back at me.

Talking about Grief

Mr. Rogers often said, "What is mentionable is manageable." This simple concept provides the framework for working with grieving children. All too often adults fear talking about death and remain silent to children's feelings and questions, leaving them overwhelmed with emotions they may not fully understand. In this developmental stage, young children see death as reversible and many times wait for their loved ones to return. This preoperational stage of childhood development can result in children feeling an over-responsibility for a loved one's illness or death.

When grieving, young children need safe spaces to explore their thoughts and feelings without judgment. *Remembering Barkley* provides this safety with simple dialogue and expressive illustrations encouraging children to share with adults. Teachable moments can spontaneously occur. Parents and professionals can provide simple ways for young people to commemorate and become recognized mourners, such as saying prayers, lighting candles, blowing bubbles, drawing "I love you" hearts, or burying dog bones.

When talking with a child, adults can follow basic guidelines for open communication, including being truthful, keeping explanations simple, sharing facts in an age-appropriate way, and reminding children the loss or death they experienced was not their fault and they did not cause it. Using age-appropriate language, such as the following definition of death, helps form these concepts: "Death is when the body stops working. Usually people die when they are very, very old, or very, very sick, or their bodies are so injured that the doctors or nurses can't make their bodies work anymore" (Goldman, *Life and Loss: A Guide to Helping Grieving Children*, 3rd edition, 2014).

Above all, we as caring adults must recognize all children grieve differently; all young people are unique, and each young person needs an avenue that promotes participation. If we strive to create a society of productive human beings, we must create evolving systems that allow children's grief to be *expressed* rather than repressed. Only then can children's internal growth light the way to emotional maturity, inner wisdom, and responsible action as universal citizens of the world.

"We are powerless to control the losses and catastrophic events our children need to experience. But by honoring their inner wisdom, providing mentors, and creating safe spaces for expression, we can empower them to become more capable, more caring, human beings" (Goldman, *Children Also Grieve: Talking about Death and Healing*, 2005).

Linda Goldman, MS, FT, LCPC, NBCC
www.grievingchildren.net